For Bridget and Kaila,
who made my incessant "why can't we have a dog?"
whine a chorus. I guess this is as close as we'll ever get.

VIKING
Published by Penguin Group
Penguin Young Readers Group
345 Hudson Street, New York, New York 10014, U.S.A.

First published in 2004 by Viking,
a division of Penguin Young Readers Group

10 9 8 7 6 5 4 3 2 1

LIBRARY OF CONGRESS CATALOGING-IN-PUBLICATION DATA
McCarthy, Meghan.
Show dog / Meghan McCarthy.
p.   cm.
Summary: When their town hosts a dog show, the Hubbles enter
their dog Ed, a lovable pooch that can spin in circles, get the news-
paper, and give big, wet, sloppy kisses.
ISBN 0-670-03688-9 (hardcover)
[1. Dogs—Fiction. 2. Dog shows—Fiction.] I. Title.
PZ7.M1282Sh 2004
[E]—dc22
2003012451

Manufactured in China
Set in Adrift
Designed by Kelley McIntyre

This is Princess. She is a show dog. Here we see her practicing for a dog show competition. Notice the perfect posture.

strong back

perfect round puffy tail

lean stomach

groomed legs

serious attitude, serious haircut

shiny teeth (even though you can't see them, believe me, they are)

clean shampooed hair

clipped nails

This is Ed. He is a show dog too.
Look at his stage presence!

dirt

ferociously
wagging tail

favorite
chewed bone

mud

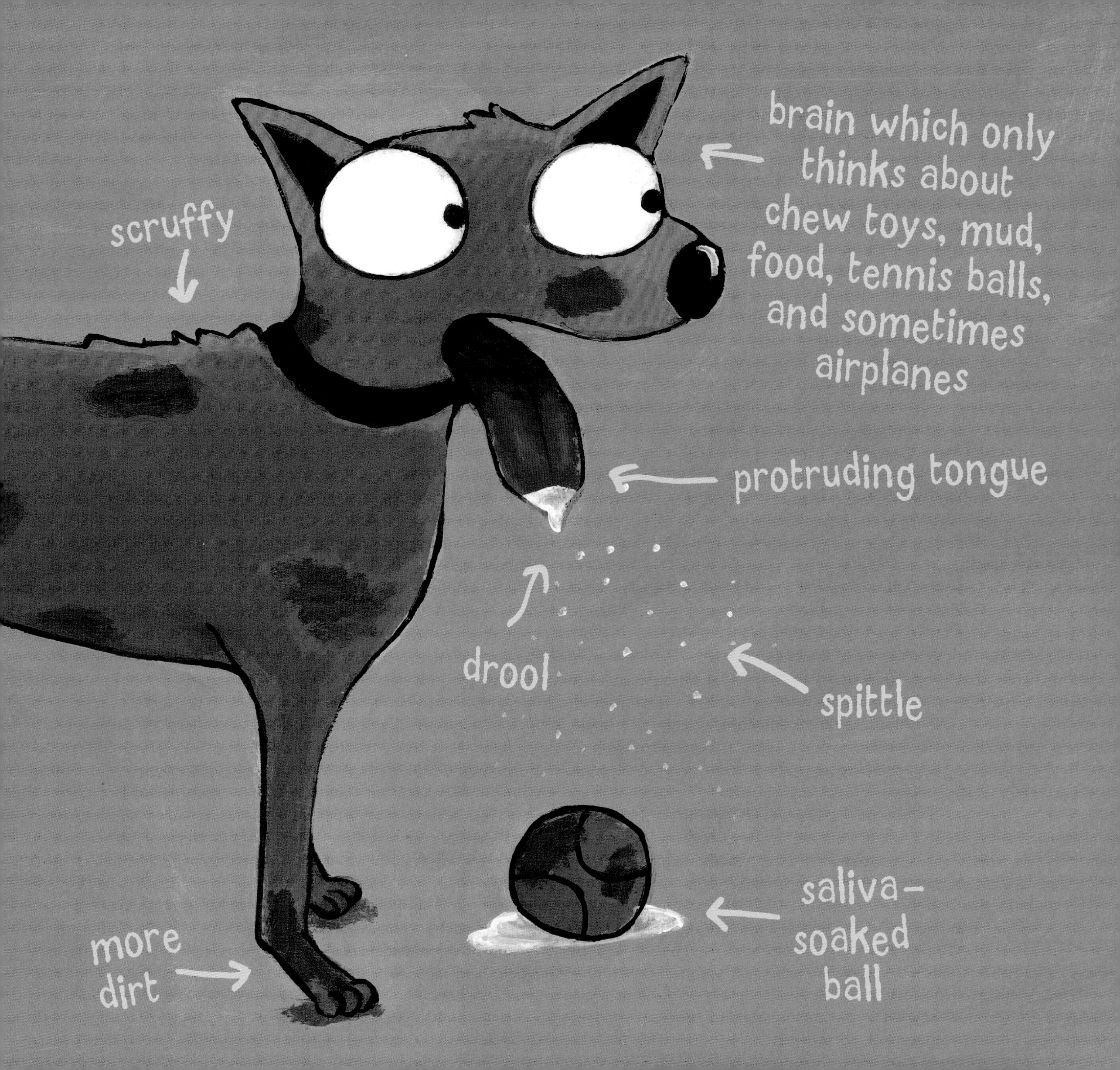
brain which only thinks about chew toys, mud, food, tennis balls, and sometimes airplanes
scruffy
protruding tongue
drool
spittle
saliva-soaked ball
more dirt

Okay, okay, so Ed isn't a show dog. But his family, the Hubbles, love him anyway. . . .

- The Hubbles -

One day, the Hubbles see an ad in the newspaper.

County Fair
DOG SHOW

Saturday ◆ 2:00 p.m.
Only the best dogs should enter, but beginners are welcome!

The Hubbles think Ed is the best dog ever.

Ed can . . .

spin in circles

get the newspaper

give big, wet kisses

He will make a great show dog.

"Show dog! Your dog isn't a show dog!" the Hubbles' neighbor, Mr. Pitt, grumbles. "My Princess is a show dog. *That* is a mangy mutt."

The Hubbles don't listen. After all, Ed
has a very good chance of winning, don't
you think? But they need to get Ed ready.
There's just one problem. . . .

They're not exactly sure what makes a dog a show dog. So they decide to find out.

They watch Princess do tricks.

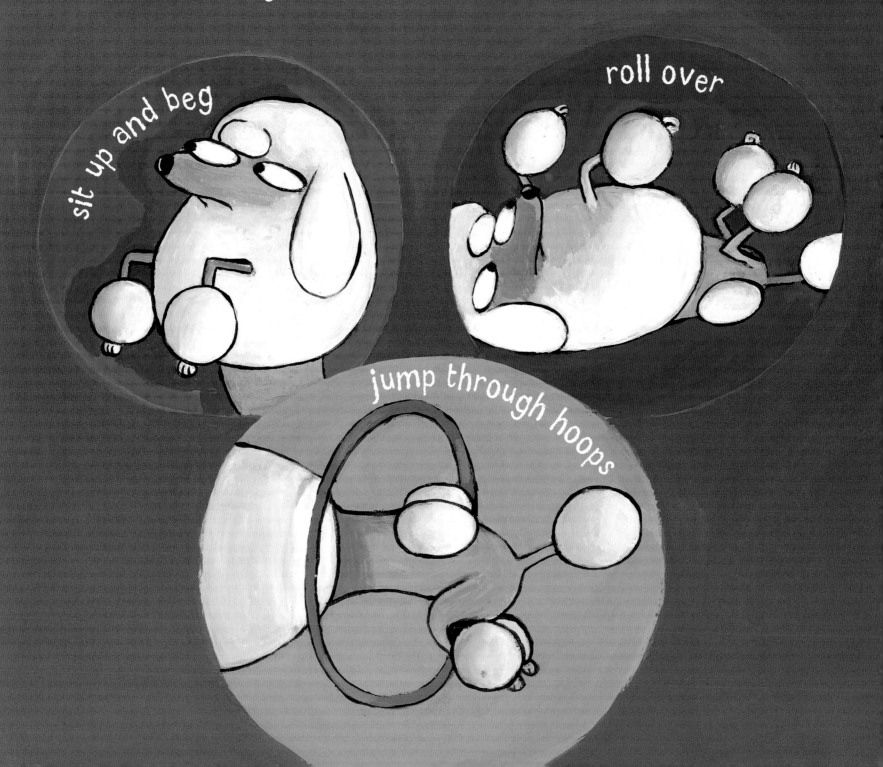

Ed does tricks too.

sit up
and beg

roll over

jump
through
hoops

Princess eats champion dog food that
makes her coat nice and shiny.

Ed does too.

Princess gets shampooed and groomed. She looks very nice and pretty, indeed.

Ed gets shampooed and groomed too.

The long-awaited dog show competition arrives! Ed and the Hubbles are very excited. The dogs parade into the arena in a perfectly straight line.

Ed does too . . . sort of.

It's time for the dogs to strut their stuff. Mr. Pitt and Princess go first. But Ed is a bit eager. He thinks it's time to play. . . .

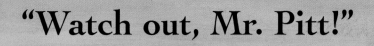

"Watch out, Mr. Pitt!"

"Your dog has ruined the show!" shouts Mr. Pitt.
Of course, the Hubbles don't listen. They think
Ed is a great dog. He can still win, right?

Wrong! The judge announces the winners.
Sheila the Shih Tzu wins third place.
Miss Lisa the Afghan Hound wins
second, and Princess the Poodle
wins first . . . but, hey!

Where is Princess? Where is Ed?
Where are the Hubbles? Where
could they possibly be?

Out celebrating, of course! Princess deserves a festive first-place dinner. And Ed does too, since he's still the best dog ever.

At least the Hubbles think so.

Princess and Ed and the Hubbles now
live happily ever after.

Mr. Pitt does NOT live happily ever after, but that's another story.

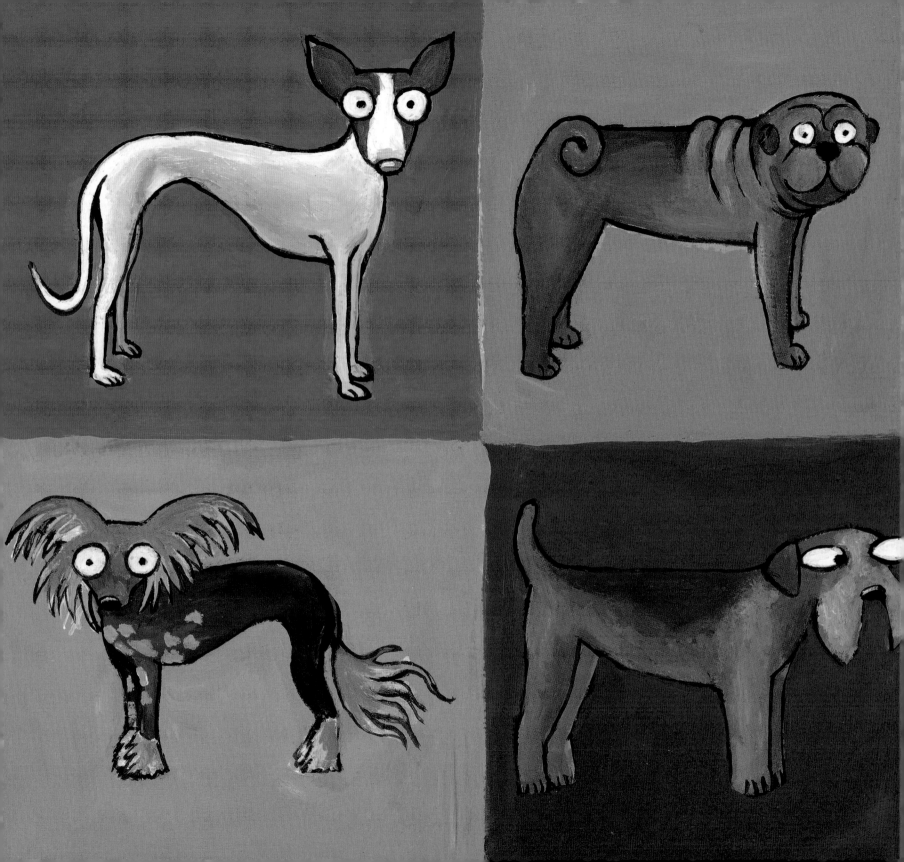